Two Golden Heart's

Soha Iman

Published by Soha Iman, 2024.

TWO GOLDEN HEART'S

First edition. August 22, 2024.

Copyright © 2024 Soha Iman.

ISBN: 979-8227155337

Written by Soha Iman.

Also by Soha Iman

Two Golden Heart's
Two Golden Heart's
Agent Alina

Episode 1: The Introduction**

—-

The sun was setting over the city, casting a warm, golden hue across the skyline. Liza stood on the rooftop of her apartment building, leaning against the railing as she looked out at the sprawling metropolis below. The wind teased her dark hair, lifting it off her shoulders in gentle waves. There was something about this time of day that always brought her a sense of peace. It was the moment when the chaos of the day started to fade, leaving behind a quiet stillness that allowed her to reflect.

Liza was known around town as a woman with a sharp tongue and an even sharper mind. At twenty-four, she had already made a name for herself as someone who didn't take nonsense from anyone. Whether it was at work or in her personal life, Liza had a reputation for being tough. But those who knew her well understood that her tough exterior was reserved only for people who deserved it. She wasn't mean-spirited or cruel; she simply didn't tolerate bad behavior, especially not from those who thought they could walk over others.

To her friends and family, Liza was a completely different person. They saw her softer side, the part of her that was fiercely loyal and deeply loving. Her attitude was a shield, one that protected those she cared about from harm. It was a quality that made her both respected and feared, depending on which side of her you were on.

Liza's family was the most important thing in her life. Growing up in a close-knit household, she had learned early on the value of sticking together. Her parents had instilled in her the belief that family came first, no matter what. And so, Liza had always been there for her family, supporting them through thick and thin. She had two younger brothers, Mark and David, who looked up to her as both a protector and a role model. They knew that no one could mess with them as long as Liza was around.

Her friends were like an extension of her family. Liza had a small but tight-knit circle of friends who had been with her through various stages of her life. They had seen her at her best and worst, and they loved her for who she was, attitude and all. Among them was Lee Yuan, a guy she had known since college.

Lee was different from anyone Liza had ever met. Where she was fiery and quick-tempered, Lee was calm and composed. He had a maturity about him that was beyond his years, and he carried himself with a quiet confidence that was both attractive and reassuring. Lee had a way of seeing the good in people, even when they didn't see it in themselves. This quality had drawn Liza to him from the moment they met.

They had become fast friends during their first year of college. Liza, who had been struggling with the pressures of a new environment and demanding coursework, found comfort in Lee's steady presence. He had a way of making everything seem manageable, even when it felt like the world was closing in on her. Over time, their friendship deepened, and they became inseparable. They were often seen together, whether it was studying in the library, grabbing coffee between classes, or just hanging out at one of their favorite spots on campus.

Now, two years after graduating, their friendship was still as strong as ever. Lee had become a constant in Liza's life, someone she could always rely on. He was the one who could make her laugh when she was feeling down, the one who would listen without judgment when she needed to vent, and the one who would stand by her side, no matter what.

But lately, Liza had started to notice something shifting between them. It was subtle at first—an extra heartbeat when their eyes met, a lingering touch when they said goodbye, a flutter in her stomach when he smiled at her in that special way. It was as if something more than friendship was simmering beneath the surface, waiting to be acknowledged.

Liza had always prided herself on being in control of her emotions, but this was different. She found herself thinking about Lee more often, wondering what it would be like to be with him in a different way. She imagined what it would feel like to hold his hand, to kiss him, to be close to him in a way that went beyond friendship. It was a thought that both excited and terrified her.

The problem was, Liza had no idea how Lee felt. He had never given any indication that he saw her as more than a friend. He was always sweet and caring, but that was just who he was. Lee treated everyone with kindness, and Liza had always assumed that was all it was—kindness. But now, she wasn't so sure. There were moments when she caught him looking at her with an intensity that made her heart skip a beat. Moments when his touch lingered a little longer than necessary, or when he seemed to be holding something back, as if he wanted to say more but wasn't sure how.

Liza was no stranger to relationships. She had dated a few guys in the past, but none of those relationships had ever felt like this. With Lee, everything was different. There was a comfort and familiarity between them that she had never experienced with anyone else. But there was also a tension, a spark that had always been there but was now starting to grow into something more.

As the sun dipped below the horizon, Liza sighed and turned away from the railing. She wasn't used to feeling this way—uncertain, vulnerable, unsure of what to do. For someone who was always so in control, it was a strange and unsettling experience. But if there was one thing Liza knew, it was that she couldn't keep ignoring her feelings. Sooner or later, she would have to confront them, and when that time came, she would need to be ready.

—-

The next day, Liza met up with Lee for lunch at their favorite café. It was a small, cozy place tucked away on a quiet street, far from the bustling crowds of the city. The café had become their go-to spot over the years, a place where they could unwind and talk without interruption.

As they sat down at their usual table by the window, Liza couldn't help but notice how comfortable it felt to be with Lee. They didn't need to fill the silence with meaningless chatter; just being in each other's presence was enough. It was something Liza cherished about their friendship—the ease with which they could be together without the pressure to constantly entertain each other.

"So, how's work been?" Lee asked as he took a sip of his coffee. He had always been good at reading Liza's mood, and today was no different. He could tell she had something on her mind, but he didn't push. Instead, he started with something familiar, something that would help her relax.

"Same old," Liza replied with a shrug. "Busy, but nothing I can't handle. You know how it is."

Lee nodded, his eyes never leaving hers. "Yeah, I get it. It's been pretty hectic on my end too. But hey, at least it's Friday, right? Got any plans for the weekend?"

Liza smiled. "Not really. Probably just catch up on some sleep, maybe hang out with the family. What about you?"

"I'm supposed to meet up with a few friends tomorrow," Lee said, leaning back in his chair. "But other than that, I'm free. We could do something if you're up for it."

Liza hesitated for a moment. The idea of spending more time with Lee was appealing, but it also made her nervous. She wasn't sure if she was ready to confront her feelings just yet. But then again, maybe spending more time together would help her figure things out.

Episode 2

"Sure," she said finally. "That sounds good. We could go to that new art exhibit everyone's been talking about."

Lee's face lit up. "That's a great idea! I've been meaning to check it out. It'll be fun."

They spent the rest of their lunch chatting about the exhibit, their conversation flowing easily as it always did. But underneath the surface, Liza's mind was racing. She kept replaying their interactions over the past few weeks, trying to find clues that might reveal how Lee felt about her. Was she imagining the connection between them, or was there really something there? And if there was, what should she do about it?

After lunch, they parted ways, each heading back to their respective jobs. As Liza walked back to her office, she couldn't shake the feeling that something was about to change. It was as if the universe was nudging her in a certain direction, urging her to take a leap of faith. But taking that leap meant risking their friendship, and that was something Liza wasn't sure she was ready to do.

The weekend came, and with it, the long-awaited visit to the art exhibit. Liza and Lee met up on Saturday afternoon, both excited to spend the day together. The exhibit was being held at a well-known gallery in the city, featuring works from a variety of contemporary artists. The theme of the exhibit was "Reflections," and it explored the ways in which artists captured and interpreted the world around them.

As they walked through the gallery, Liza found herself drawn to a particular painting. It was an abstract piece, full of vibrant colors and bold brushstrokes. The artist had used a combination of light and shadow to create a sense of depth and movement, making the painting feel almost alive.

"This one's interesting," Liza said, tilting her head as she studied the painting. "It's like the artist is trying to convey something beyond what's on the surface. There's an energy to it, something that pulls you in."

Lee stepped up beside her, his eyes scanning the painting.

He said you are a bad painter

Liza said yeah if I am bad then what about you Yuan smiled and said I was just kidding

You are an amazing painter.

Liza was never one to back down from a challenge, especially when it came to standing up against injustice. She had always believed that bad people needed to be put in their place, and she wasn't afraid to be the one to do it. Over the years, she had developed a reputation as someone you didn't want to mess with. But while some might see her as confrontational, those close to her understood that Liza's attitude wasn't born out of malice—it was a protective instinct, honed over years of watching people she cared about get hurt.

It was a Tuesday afternoon when Liza's protective instincts were put to the test once again. She was at work, sitting at her desk and going over some reports, when she overheard a conversation between two of her coworkers, Jenna and Rick. Rick was one of those guys who always seemed to think he was better than everyone else. He was arrogant, condescending, and often made snide remarks that rubbed people the wrong way. Liza had managed to avoid most of his nonsense, but today, he had crossed a line.

"I'm just saying, Jenna," Rick's voice carried over from the next cubicle. "If you want to be taken seriously around here, you need to stop dressing like that. It's unprofessional."

Liza's ears perked up, and she felt her blood begin to boil. Jenna was one of the sweetest people in the office, always kind and considerate, and she didn't deserve to be talked to like that. Liza stood up from her desk and walked over to where Jenna and Rick were standing. She could see the hurt in Jenna's eyes as she tried to defend herself, but Rick wasn't backing down.

"Rick," Liza said, her voice steady but with a hint of warning, "do you have a problem with the way Jenna dresses?"

Rick turned to look at Liza, clearly surprised by her sudden appearance. "Liza, I was just giving her some friendly advice. No need to get involved."

"Oh, I think there is," Liza replied, crossing her arms. "Because it sounds to me like you're being a jerk. Jenna doesn't need your 'advice' on how to dress. She's perfectly capable of making her own decisions."

Rick scoffed, clearly not taking Liza seriously. "Look, I'm just trying to help. If she wants to be respected in the office, she needs to look the part."

"And who exactly made you the authority on what's professional?" Liza shot back. "Last I checked, we're all here to do our jobs, not to judge each other's appearance. If you have a problem with that, maybe you're the one who needs to rethink your attitude."

By now, a few other coworkers had gathered around, curious about the confrontation. Liza could feel their eyes on her, but she didn't care. She was focused on Rick, who was starting to realize that he wasn't going to win this argument.

"Fine," Rick muttered, clearly annoyed. "Whatever. It's not a big deal."

"Oh, it is a big deal," Liza replied, her voice firm. "Because this isn't the first time you've made someone feel uncomfortable with your comments. It needs to stop, Rick. You need to start treating people with respect, or you're going to find yourself very alone around here."

Rick didn't say anything, but the look on his face told Liza that he had gotten the message. He turned and walked away, clearly frustrated but unwilling to push the issue any further. Liza watched him go before turning to Jenna, who was still standing there, looking a little shaken.

"Are you okay?" Liza asked, her voice softening.

Jenna nodded, though she still looked upset. "Yeah, I'm fine. Thanks for stepping in, Liza. I didn't know what to say to him."

"You don't need to thank me," Liza replied, giving her a reassuring smile. "He was out of line, and someone needed to put him in his place. If he ever gives you trouble again, just let me know."

Jenna smiled back, clearly grateful for Liza's support. "I will. Thanks, Liza."

Liza nodded and gave her a gentle pat on the shoulder before heading back to her desk. She could feel the eyes of her coworkers on her as she walked, but she didn't mind. If standing up to people like Rick made her unpopular with certain folks, so be it. She wasn't in this job to make friends with everyone—she was here to do her work and make sure that the people she cared about were treated with the respect they deserved.

Later that evening, Liza met up with Lee at their usual spot—a small, quiet park not far from her apartment. It was their go-to place to unwind after a long day, and tonight, Liza needed it more than ever. She was still fuming over the incident with Rick, and she knew that talking to Lee would help her calm down.

When she arrived, Lee was already there, sitting on one of the benches with a book in his hands. He looked up as she approached, his face lighting up with a smile.

"Hey," he greeted her as she sat down next to him. "You look like you've had a rough day."

"You could say that," Liza replied, leaning back against the bench. She let out a long sigh, trying to release some of the tension that had built up in her shoulders. "It's just been one of those days, you know? Dealing with people who think they're better than everyone else."

Lee nodded, setting his book aside. "Want to talk about it?"

Liza glanced at him, grateful as always for his calm presence. "Yeah, I think I do. There's this guy at work, Rick. He's always making these snide comments, like he thinks he's doing everyone a favor by criticizing them. Today, he said something to Jenna about the way she dresses, and it just... it just pissed me off."

"I can see why," Lee said, his expression serious. "That's not okay. Did you confront him?"

"Of course I did," Liza replied, a hint of pride in her voice. "I told him off in front of everyone. He backed down, but I could tell he was annoyed. I just don't get why some people think it's okay to put others down like that. It's like they get some kind of sick pleasure out of it."

Lee nodded again, his eyes thoughtful. "Some people are just insecure, Liza. They feel the need to belittle others to make themselves feel better. It's not right, but unfortunately, it happens."

"I know," Liza said with a sigh. "I just can't stand it when people treat others like they're less than. It's not fair."

"No, it's not," Lee agreed. "But I'm glad you stood up for Jenna. It's important to have people like you who aren't afraid to speak out when something's wrong."

Liza smiled at him, feeling a warmth spread through her chest. Lee always had a way of making her feel better, even when she was at her most frustrated. "Thanks, Lee. I don't know what I'd do without you."

"You'd be just fine," Lee replied with a chuckle. "But I'm glad to be here for you, all the same."

They sat in comfortable silence for a few moments, watching as the last light of the day faded into dusk. The park was quiet, with only the occasional sound of birds chirping or leaves rustling in the breeze. Liza felt herself starting to relax, the tension from the day slowly melting away.

"You know," Lee said after a while, breaking the silence, "you're pretty amazing, Liza."

Liza looked at him, surprised. "What do you mean?"

"I mean," Lee continued, "that you have this incredible ability to stand up for what's right, even when it's not easy. A lot of people would have just ignored Rick or let it slide, but you didn't. You spoke up, and you made a difference. That's not something everyone can do."

Liza felt her cheeks flush at the compliment. "I don't know about that. I just do what I think is right."

"And that's what makes you amazing," Lee said, his voice sincere. "You don't just talk about what's right—you act on it. You're not afraid to take a stand, even if it means making enemies. That's something I really admire about you."

Liza felt a warmth spread through her chest at his words. She had always known that Lee respected her, but hearing him say it out loud, especially in such a heartfelt way, meant more to her than she could express.

"Thanks, Lee," she said softly, meeting his gaze. "That really means a lot to me."

Lee smiled at her, his eyes filled with affection. "Anytime, Liza. You know I'm always here for you."

Liza felt a surge of emotion as she looked at him, her heart swelling with affection. She had always known that Lee was special, but moments like this reminded her just how much he meant to her.

He wasn't just a friend—he was someone who truly understood her, someone who appreciated her for who she was, attitude and all.

As they sat together, the sky above them darkening into night, Liza couldn't help but wonder what it would be like to take their relationship to the next level. The thought of being with Lee in a romantic way had been lingering in her mind more and more lately, and tonight, it felt closer than ever.

But she also knew that making such

Episode 3

Episode 3: The Turning Point

Liza couldn't shake the feeling of uncertainty that had settled in her chest since that evening in the park with Lee. The more she thought about his words, the more they played on her mind. For the first time, she found herself questioning the boundaries of their friendship and wondering if there was something more between them. She had never been one to second-guess herself, but when it came to Lee, everything felt different.

It was Thursday morning, and Liza was getting ready for work when her phone buzzed with a message from Lee.

Lee: *Hey, I'm grabbing coffee before work. Want to join?*

Liza smiled at the screen. She didn't have to be at the office for another hour, and the idea of spending time with Lee sounded like the perfect way to start her day.

Liza: *Sure! Meet you at the usual spot?*

Lee: *You got it. See you in 15.*

Liza quickly finished getting ready and headed out the door. The café where they usually met was just a short walk from her apartment, and by the time she arrived, Lee was already there, waiting for her with a coffee in hand.

"Morning," he greeted her with a smile, handing her the cup. "I got your favorite."

"Thanks," Liza said, taking the coffee and feeling a little flutter in her stomach at the simple, thoughtful gesture. "You always know how to start my day off right."

"Just trying to keep you happy," Lee replied with a playful grin as they sat down at one of the tables near the window.

They chatted casually as they sipped their coffee, talking about their plans for the day and anything else that came to mind. But beneath the lighthearted conversation, Liza could feel the tension building inside her. She knew she had to talk to Lee about the way she was feeling, but she didn't know how to bring it up. What if he didn't feel the same way? What if bringing it up ruined the easy, comfortable friendship they had built over the years?

As they finished their coffee and prepared to head to work, Liza knew she couldn't keep avoiding the subject. She had to find out where they stood, even if it meant risking everything.

"Lee," she said as they walked out of the café, her voice hesitant. "Can I ask you something?"

"Of course," Lee replied, his expression turning serious as he noticed the change in her tone. "What's on your mind?"

Liza took a deep breath, gathering her courage. "Do you ever... I mean, have you ever thought about us as more than friends?"

Lee stopped in his tracks, turning to look at her with surprise. For a moment, he didn't say anything, and Liza's heart pounded in her chest as she waited for his response.

"Honestly, Liza," he began slowly, his voice careful, "I've thought about it. I'd be lying if I said I hadn't."

Liza felt her breath catch. "You have?"

Lee nodded, his gaze steady. "Yeah. I mean, we've been through so much together, and you're one of the most important people in my life. I've wondered what it would be like if we were more than friends. But I've never wanted to push it, because our friendship means too much to me. I didn't want to risk losing what we have."

Liza's mind was racing. She had expected the conversation to be difficult, but she hadn't anticipated how vulnerable she would feel hearing Lee's honest admission. Part of her wanted to jump at the opportunity to explore their feelings, but another part of her was terrified of what it could mean for their relationship.

"I feel the same way," Liza confessed, her voice barely above a whisper. "Lately, I've been thinking about it more and more, and I can't help but wonder if we're... I don't know, meant to be something more."

Lee reached out, gently taking her hand in his. The touch sent a jolt of electricity through Liza, and she looked up to meet his gaze.

"Liza," he said softly, "you know I care about you more than anything. But this is a big step, and I want to make sure we're both on the same page. I don't want to rush into something just because it feels right in the moment. If we're going to do this, we need to be sure."

Liza nodded, understanding the weight of his words. Lee was always the steady one, the one who thought things through before making a decision. It was one of the things she loved about him, and she knew he was right. They couldn't just dive into a relationship without considering the impact it would have on their friendship.

"You're right," she agreed, squeezing his hand. "I don't want to lose what we have, Lee. But I also don't want to ignore how I feel. Maybe we just need to take things slow, figure it out as we go."

Lee smiled, a look of relief crossing his face. "I think that's a good idea. Let's take our time and see where this goes. No pressure, no expectations—just us."

Liza felt a sense of peace settle over her. She didn't have all the answers, but she didn't need them right now. What mattered was that they were both willing to explore this new territory together, and that was enough for her.

"Okay," she said, smiling back at him. "Let's see where this goes."

The next few weeks were a whirlwind of emotions for Liza and Lee. They continued to spend time together, just as they always had, but there was a new undercurrent to their interactions—an unspoken understanding that something had shifted between them.

Liza found herself looking forward to their time together even more than before, savoring every moment they spent in each other's company. Whether they were out with friends, working together on a project, or just hanging out at one of their favorite spots, there was a new level of intimacy that hadn't been there before. It was as if they were both more attuned to each other, more aware of the little things that made their relationship special.

But along with the excitement came moments of doubt and uncertainty. Liza couldn't help but wonder if they were doing the right thing, if exploring this new dynamic would ultimately bring them closer or drive them apart. There were times when she questioned whether she was ready to take that leap, whether she was prepared for the possibility that things might not work out the way she hoped.

One evening, as they were sitting in Liza's apartment watching a movie, Lee turned to her, a thoughtful expression on his face.

"Liza, can I ask you something?" he said, his voice soft.

"Of course," Liza replied, pausing the movie and turning to face him.

"I've been thinking a lot about us lately," Lee began, his tone serious. "And I guess I just want to know... what do you really want out of this? I mean, where do you see this going?"

Liza was taken aback by the question, but she knew it was one they needed to address. She had been so focused on her own feelings that she hadn't stopped to consider what Lee wanted, what he was hoping to get out of this new chapter in their relationship.

"I don't know," Liza admitted, her voice tinged with uncertainty. "I've never really thought about it in concrete terms. I guess I've just been going with the flow, trying to figure things out as we go."

Lee nodded, his expression thoughtful. "I get that. But I think we need to be honest with each other about what we want. If we're going to make this work, we need to make sure we're both on the same page."

Liza felt a pang of anxiety at his words. She wasn't used to being this vulnerable, to laying all her cards on the table and admitting that she didn't have all the answers. But she also knew that Lee was right—they couldn't move forward without being honest with each other.

"I want to be with you, Lee," she said finally, her voice firm despite the butterflies in her stomach. "I don't know exactly what that looks like yet, but I know that I care about you, and I want to see where this goes."

Lee's expression softened, and he reached out to take her hand in his. "That's all I needed to hear, Liza. I care about you too, more than I can put into words. And I want to be with you, whatever that means for us. We don't have to have all the answers right now. We just need to be open and honest with each other, and we'll figure it out together."

Liza felt a wave of relief wash over her. She hadn't realized how much she needed to hear those words until now. Lee's reassurance gave her the confidence to move forward, to embrace this new chapter in their lives with an open heart.

"Okay," she said, smiling at him. "We'll figure it out together."

Episode 4

Over the next few days, Liza and Lee settled into a new rhythm, one that felt both familiar and excitingly different. They continued to spend time together, but there was a new sense of purpose in their interactions, a shared understanding that they were building something more than just a friendship.

One evening, as they were walking through the city after dinner, Lee turned to Liza with a mischievous grin.

"You know," he said, his tone playful, "I've been thinking…"

"Oh, no," Liza teased, nudging him with her elbow. "That's never a good sign."

Lee laughed, his eyes sparkling with the warmth Liza had grown so fond of. "Hey, I do my best thinking when I'm with you," he retorted, playfully bumping her shoulder with his.

Liza chuckled, feeling a familiar flutter in her chest at his light-hearted banter. "Alright, alright. What have you been thinking about, genius?"

"Well," Lee began, his tone growing more serious as they continued walking down the softly lit street, "I was thinking about how we've been figuring things out, taking things slow. And I love that we're both being careful about this, but… I also think we deserve to have some fun while we're at it."

Liza raised an eyebrow, intrigued. "Fun, huh? What do you have in mind?"

"How about a proper date?" Lee suggested, his grin widening. "I mean, a real one. No casual hangouts, no group dinners—just you and me, going somewhere special."

Liza felt a rush of excitement at the idea. They'd been spending time together as usual, but calling it a date made it feel different—more intentional. It was a step forward, and one she realized she was more than ready to take.

"I like the sound of that," Liza admitted, her voice tinged with enthusiasm. "So, what do you have in mind?"

"I was thinking we could keep it simple but meaningful," Lee said, his eyes meeting hers. "There's this new art exhibit opening at the museum. I know how much you love art, and I thought it might be a nice change of pace."

Liza's heart swelled at his thoughtfulness. He had remembered her love for art, something they hadn't talked about in a while. The idea of sharing that with him, of experiencing something she loved with someone who meant so much to her, filled her with anticipation.

"That sounds perfect," Liza said, smiling at him. "When do you want to go?"

"How about this Saturday?" Lee suggested. "We can grab dinner afterward, make a whole evening of it."

"It's a date," Liza agreed, feeling a mixture of excitement and nervousness settle in her stomach. This was it—an official step toward something more.

Saturday arrived with a sense of anticipation that Liza hadn't felt in a long time. She spent the day carefully choosing her outfit, wanting to strike the right balance between casual and special. She finally settled on a deep blue dress that brought out the color of her eyes, paired with a light cardigan and her favorite ankle boots. As she looked at herself in the mirror, she felt a wave of nerves wash over her. This wasn't just any other day with Lee—this was a date, and the weight of that realization made her heart race.

When Lee arrived at her apartment to pick her up, Liza couldn't help but notice how handsome he looked. He was wearing a neatly pressed shirt and dark jeans, his hair slightly tousled in that effortlessly charming way he always seemed to pull off. As he smiled at her, she felt her nerves start to melt away, replaced by a warm sense of excitement.

"You look amazing," Lee said, his voice filled with genuine admiration as he took her in.

"Thanks," Liza replied, feeling a blush creep up her cheeks. "You don't look so bad yourself."

They shared a smile before heading out, the cool evening air filled with the promise of a memorable night. The museum wasn't far, and they decided to walk, enjoying the comfortable silence that had always been a part of their dynamic. But tonight, the silence felt different—charged with unspoken possibilities.

When they arrived at the museum, Liza was struck by how beautiful it looked at night. The building was bathed in soft lights, and the air was filled with the faint sounds of classical music drifting from inside. As they entered, Liza felt a sense of calm settle over her. Being in a place filled with art always had that effect on her, and sharing it with Lee made it even more special.

They wandered through the exhibit, taking in the paintings and sculptures, each piece sparking conversations that flowed effortlessly between them. Liza found herself getting lost in the art, but every time she glanced at Lee, she was reminded of why this night was different. He wasn't just her friend tonight—he was someone she was beginning to see in a new light, someone who made her feel more alive than she had in a long time.

As they moved through the exhibit, they found themselves in front of a particularly striking painting—a vibrant, swirling mix of colors that seemed to pulse with energy.

"Wow," Liza breathed, staring at the painting in awe. "It's incredible."

"It really is," Lee agreed, standing close beside her. "It reminds me of you, actually."

Liza turned to him, surprised. "What do you mean?"

Lee smiled, his eyes soft as he looked at her. "It's bold and dynamic, full of life and energy—just like you. And just like the painting, there's something about you that draws people in, that makes them want to be around you."

Liza felt her heart skip a beat at his words. She had always known Lee cared about her, but hearing him express it so openly, so sincerely, made her realize just how deep his feelings might go.

"Lee," she said softly, her voice barely above a whisper. "I—"

Before she could finish, Lee gently took her hand, his touch sending a jolt of warmth through her. "Liza," he said, his voice low and filled with emotion, "I've been thinking a lot about what you said the other day, about wanting to see where this goes. And I've realized something—I don't want to just see where this goes. I want to be with you. I don't want to hold back anymore."

Liza felt a rush of emotions as his words sank in. This was the moment she had been waiting for, the moment when they could finally stop dancing around their feelings and just be honest with each other.

"I want that too, Lee," she said, her voice trembling with emotion. "I've been scared, but the truth is, I care about you more than I've ever cared about anyone. And I don't want to hold back either."

Lee's smile widened, and in that moment, Liza felt like the world had narrowed down to just the two of them. Everything else faded away—the museum, the people around them, even the painting they had been admiring. All that mattered was Lee, and the way he was looking at her, with a depth of feeling that took her breath away.

Without another word, Lee gently cupped her face in his hands and leaned in, his lips brushing against hers in a tender, hesitant kiss.

The touch was soft at first, almost tentative, but as Liza responded, it deepened into something more, something that felt like the culmination of everything they had been building toward.

The kiss was both a promise and a new beginning—a way of saying that they were in this together, no matter what the future held. When they finally pulled apart, Liza felt like she was floating, her heart soaring with a happiness she hadn't known she was capable of.

"I've wanted to do that for so long," Lee admitted, his forehead resting against hers.

"Me too," Liza whispered, her eyes closed as she savored the moment. "I'm so glad we finally did."

Episode 5

Navigating New Territory**

—-

The days following their first official date were a blend of excitement and subtle changes for Liza and Lee. While the foundation of their friendship remained strong, their relationship had taken on a new depth. The transition from best friends to something more was both thrilling and a little daunting, as they navigated the uncharted waters of being together in a different way.

They continued to spend time together, but now there was an added layer of intimacy to their interactions. Little gestures—like holding hands, stolen kisses, and the way Lee would sometimes brush a stray hair from Liza's face—took on a new significance. Everything felt more deliberate, more meaningful, and Liza couldn't help but notice how much she was falling for Lee all over again, but this time, as more than just a friend.

Yet with these new emotions came moments of self-doubt. Liza found herself wondering if she was doing the right thing, if she was truly ready for a relationship that could potentially alter the dynamic of one of the most important friendships in her life. What if things didn't work out? What if they ended up losing everything they had built over the years? The thoughts nagged at the back of her mind, even as she continued to embrace the happiness that being with Lee brought her.

One evening, after a particularly long day at work, Liza found herself lying on her couch, staring up at the ceiling as her thoughts swirled. She was exhausted, but sleep eluded her. Instead, she kept replaying the past few weeks in her mind—their date, their conversations, and the way things had changed between them.

Her phone buzzed on the coffee table, pulling her out of her thoughts. It was a message from Lee.

Lee: *Hey, you up for a late-night chat?*

Liza smiled, grateful for the distraction. She reached for her phone and quickly typed a reply.

Liza: *Sure, what's on your mind?*

Lee's response came almost immediately.

Lee: *Actually, can I come over? I need to talk to you about something.*

Liza felt a twinge of concern at the seriousness of his tone. It wasn't like Lee to be cryptic, and the fact that he wanted to talk in person made her stomach twist with unease.

Liza: *Of course. Come over whenever.*

She put her phone down and sat up, her mind racing with possibilities. What could he need to talk about that couldn't wait until tomorrow? Was something wrong? She tried to push the anxious thoughts aside, reminding herself that whatever it was, they would deal with it together—just like they always had.

Fifteen minutes later, there was a knock at the door. Liza's heart skipped a beat as she got up to answer it. When she opened the door, Lee was standing there, looking slightly more serious than usual.

"Hey," he said, his voice soft. "Sorry to show up so late."

"Don't apologize," Liza replied, stepping aside to let him in. "You know you're always welcome."

They moved to the living room, where Lee sat down on the couch, his expression thoughtful. Liza sat beside him, waiting for him to speak. For a moment, there was silence, and Liza could feel the tension in the air.

"Liza," Lee began finally, turning to look at her, "there's something I've been thinking about, and I need to talk to you about it."

"Okay," Liza said, trying to keep her voice steady. "What is it?"

Lee took a deep breath, as if he were gathering his thoughts. "I've been thinking a lot about us, about how things have changed between us recently. And I want you to know that I'm really happy with where we are. But I've also been wondering... how do we tell everyone else?"

Liza blinked, taken aback by the question. It wasn't what she had been expecting, and she realized she hadn't really thought about it. So far, their relationship had been just between the two of them—a private, special thing that they were still figuring out. But of course, eventually, they would have to tell their friends and family.

"I hadn't really thought about it," Liza admitted, feeling a little foolish for not having considered it sooner. "I guess I was just so focused on us that I didn't think about how we'd handle it with everyone else."

Lee nodded, his expression understanding. "I get that. I've been thinking about it a lot, though, and I just want to make sure we're on the same page. I don't want to rush you into anything, but I also don't want us to feel like we're hiding, you know?"

Liza nodded, her mind racing. She could see where he was coming from—she didn't want to feel like they were keeping secrets, but she also wasn't sure how to handle the transition from best friends to a couple in the eyes of everyone else.

"Maybe we could start small," Liza suggested after a moment of thought. "We don't have to make a big announcement or anything. We could just tell a few close friends first, see how that goes, and then gradually let everyone else know."

Lee's expression softened into a smile. "I think that's a good idea. We don't have to make a big deal out of it, but I want the people who matter to us to know how much you mean to me."

Liza felt a warmth spread through her chest at his words. The way Lee was so considerate, so thoughtful about every aspect of their relationship, made her fall for him even more. She reached out and took his hand, squeezing it gently.

"You mean a lot to me too, Lee," she said, her voice filled with emotion. "And I'm really glad we're doing this together."

They sat there in comfortable silence for a while, simply holding hands and enjoying each other's presence. Liza felt the weight of her earlier doubts lift slightly, replaced by a sense of calm. She knew there would be challenges ahead, but as long as they faced them together, she was confident they could handle whatever came their way.

—-

The next day, Liza and Lee decided to start by telling one of their closest mutual friends, Sarah. Sarah had been in their friend group for years and was someone they both trusted deeply. They knew she would be supportive, and it felt like the right first step in sharing their news.

They arranged to meet her for lunch at a small café they all liked. As they sat down at a table by the window, Liza felt a mixture of excitement and nerves. She knew Sarah would be happy for them, but she couldn't shake the feeling of butterflies in her stomach.

"So," Sarah said, smiling at them as she sipped her coffee, "what's new with you two? You've both been so busy lately, I feel like we haven't caught up in ages."

Liza exchanged a quick glance with Lee, and he gave her a reassuring nod. She took a deep breath before speaking.

"Well, there's actually something we wanted to tell you," Liza began, her voice steady. "Lee and I... we've started seeing each other."

For a moment, there was silence as Sarah processed the news. Then, a wide grin spread across her face.

"Are you serious?" she exclaimed, her eyes lighting up. "Oh my gosh, I'm so happy for you guys! I always thought you'd make the perfect couple."

Liza felt a wave of relief wash over her at Sarah's reaction. She hadn't realized just how much she had been worried about how their friends would take the news until now.

"Thanks, Sarah," Lee said, smiling. "We're still figuring things out, but we didn't want to keep it a secret from you."

Sarah reached across the table and took both of their hands, her smile never fading. "I'm so glad you told me. And for what it's worth, I think you guys are going to be great together. You've always had something special, and now you get to explore that in a whole new way."

Liza felt her heart swell with gratitude. Sarah's support meant the world to her, and hearing her say those words gave her the reassurance she needed. Maybe this wouldn't be as difficult as she had feared.

They spent the rest of the lunch catching up and talking about everything from work to weekend plans. But there was an added sense of excitement in the air, a feeling that they were moving forward into a new chapter of their lives.

As they left the café, Sarah gave them both a hug, her enthusiasm infectious. "You two take care of each other, okay? And keep me updated—I want to hear all about your first official date as a couple!"

Liza laughed, feeling lighter than she had in days. "We will, promise."

—-

Over the next few weeks, Liza and Lee gradually told more of their friends about their relationship. Each time, they were met with excitement and support, and with every positive reaction, Liza's confidence in their decision grew.

However, the one person Liza hadn't told yet was her mother. Despite their close relationship, Liza felt nervous about breaking the news to her. It wasn't that she thought her mom would disapprove—far from it. Her mom had always adored Lee and had often joked that they were like an old married couple already. But something about telling her mom made everything feel more real, more permanent, and that thought was both exhilarating and a little terrifying.

One evening, Liza finally decided it was time. She invited her mom over for dinner, determined to share her news and get it over with. As she cooked, her nerves

Episode 6

Episode 4 (continued): Navigating New Territory

—-

As Liza prepared dinner, her nerves fluttered in her stomach like butterflies. She knew she had nothing to worry about—her mom adored Lee, after all—but there was something about telling her mother that made everything feel more official. Liza had always been close to her mom, and her opinion mattered deeply to her. Despite the positive reactions from her friends, this conversation felt like the final hurdle before she could fully embrace her relationship with Lee.

The doorbell rang, and Liza wiped her hands on a dish towel before heading to the door. She took a deep breath, willing herself to stay calm, and opened the door to find her mother standing there with a warm smile on her face.

"Hi, sweetie!" her mom greeted her, pulling Liza into a tight hug. "It smells wonderful in here. You've really outdone yourself."

"Thanks, Mom," Liza said, returning the hug with a smile. "Come on in, dinner's almost ready."

They settled into the kitchen, where the table was set with Liza's best dishes and a bottle of wine waited to be opened. As Liza put the finishing touches on the meal, her mom watched her with a curious expression.

"So, what's the occasion?" her mom asked, her tone light but inquisitive. "It's not often you invite me over for a fancy dinner like this."

Liza bit her lip, feeling a surge of nerves. This was it—the moment she had been both anticipating and dreading. She knew she couldn't put it off any longer, so she took a deep breath and turned to face her mom.

"There's actually something I wanted to talk to you about," Liza began, trying to keep her voice steady. "It's about Lee."

Her mom's expression softened immediately, her smile growing. "Lee? What about him? Is everything okay?"

Liza nodded, feeling her heart race. "Yes, everything's fine. It's just... well, Lee and I have started seeing each other. Like, in a romantic way."

There was a brief moment of silence as her mom processed the news. Then, a slow smile spread across her face, her eyes twinkling with warmth.

"Oh, Liza," her mom said, her voice filled with genuine happiness. "That's wonderful news! I've always thought you two were perfect for each other. I'm so happy for you both."

Liza felt a wave of relief wash over her, the tension in her shoulders easing. She had known her mom would be supportive, but hearing it out loud made all the difference.

"Thanks, Mom," Liza said, smiling back at her. "We've been taking things slow, but it feels right. I just wanted you to know."

Her mom reached across the counter and took Liza's hand, giving it a reassuring squeeze. "I'm so proud of you, Liza. You've always known what's best for you, and I'm glad you and Lee are exploring this together. He's a good man, and I know he'll take care of you."

Liza felt tears prick at the corners of her eyes, her emotions swelling at her mom's kind words. "I'm really happy, Mom," she admitted, her voice thick with emotion. "It's like everything is finally falling into place."

"I can see that," her mom replied, her smile never fading. "And that's all I've ever wanted for you—for you to be happy. You and Lee have been through so much together, and I'm sure this new chapter will be just as special."

They sat down to dinner, and the conversation flowed easily, with Liza's mom asking about how things had progressed between her and Lee. Liza found herself opening up more than she had expected, sharing the little moments that had led to their relationship and how she felt about this new territory they were navigating.

By the end of the meal, Liza felt lighter, as if a weight she hadn't even realized she was carrying had been lifted. Her mom's support meant the world to her, and now that she had it, she felt ready to fully embrace this new chapter with Lee.

—-

In the days that followed, Liza and Lee continued to grow closer, their relationship blossoming in ways that surprised them both. The transition from friends to a couple was smoother than they had anticipated, and the deep bond they already shared made everything feel natural.

But as their relationship deepened, Liza began to notice subtle changes in her interactions with others, particularly when it came to people outside their close-knit circle of friends. It wasn't that anyone was overtly unkind or disapproving, but there were moments—small, fleeting ones—that made Liza realize how different things were now that she and Lee were together.

One afternoon, while Liza was at work, she ran into an old acquaintance, Julia, in the break room. Julia had been in a few of Liza's classes in college, and though they hadn't been close friends, they had always gotten along well enough. They exchanged pleasantries, catching up on work and life in general, before Julia's expression turned a little more curious.

"So, I heard you and Lee are a thing now," Julia said, her tone light but with a hint of something else—something Liza couldn't quite put her finger on.

Liza smiled, nodding. "Yeah, we are. It's still pretty new, but it's going really well."

Julia raised an eyebrow, her smile a little too knowing. "That's great. I always wondered when you two would finally get together. I mean, you've been best friends forever, right? It was only a matter of time."

Liza felt a twinge of discomfort at Julia's words. She knew Julia didn't mean anything by it, but the implication that their relationship was inevitable, that it had been predestined because of their friendship, rubbed her the wrong way. It made their relationship feel less like a choice and more like a foregone conclusion.

"Yeah, we've known each other for a long time," Liza said, keeping her tone neutral. "But it wasn't something we planned. It just... happened when the time was right."

Julia nodded, her smile still in place. "Well, good for you guys. I'm sure it'll work out. You two were always so close—it makes sense you'd end up together."

Liza forced a smile, feeling a wave of irritation she couldn't quite shake. She didn't want to get into a debate about her relationship with someone who wasn't even a close friend, so she kept her response polite and brief.

"Thanks, Julia. I appreciate it."

As they wrapped up their conversation and went their separate ways, Liza couldn't help but replay the interaction in her mind. Julia hadn't said anything overtly negative, but the way she had framed their relationship as something inevitable, something almost expected, bothered Liza more than she cared to admit.

Later that evening, when she met up with Lee for dinner, she found herself bringing up the conversation.

"I ran into Julia today," Liza said as they sat down at their favorite restaurant. "She made some comments that got me thinking."

Lee looked at her curiously, his brow furrowing slightly. "What did she say?"

Liza sighed, swirling her drink around in her glass before taking a sip. "She basically said that our relationship was inevitable, that it was only a matter of time before we got together because we were so close as friends."

Lee's expression softened with understanding. "And that bothered you?"

"A little," Liza admitted. "I know she didn't mean anything by it, but it made me feel like our relationship isn't being seen as a choice we made, but as something that was bound to happen. Like we didn't have a say in it."

Lee reached across the table and took her hand, his touch grounding her. "I get it, Liza. But we both know that's not true. We chose this. We chose each other, and that's what matters. No one else's opinions or assumptions can change that."

Liza felt a sense of relief wash over her at his words. He was right—what mattered was the choice they had made, together. And that was something no one else could take away from them.

"Thanks, Lee," Liza said, squeezing his hand. "I needed to hear that."

"Anytime," Lee replied with a smile. "And for what it's worth, I'm glad we made that choice. Being with you... it's better than I ever imagined."

Liza felt her heart swell with affection for him. "Me too, Lee. Me too."

—-

As time passed, Liza and Lee grew more comfortable in their new roles as a couple. They continued to navigate the ups and downs of their relationship with the same openness and honesty that had always defined their friendship.

But as they settled into their new dynamic, Liza began to realize that being in a relationship with someone you've known for so long comes with its own unique set of challenges. While they had always been open with each other, there were still aspects of their lives—past experiences, insecurities, and dreams—that they hadn't fully shared. And now that they were more than friends, those unspoken parts of their lives became more significant.

One evening, as they were sitting on Liza's couch watching a movie, Lee suddenly turned to her, his expression thoughtful.

"Liza," he began, his voice soft, "can I ask you something?"

"Of course," Liza replied, pausing the movie and giving him her full attention. "What's on your mind?"

Lee hesitated for a moment, as if he were trying to find the right words. "I've been thinking a lot about

Episode 7

Episode 7 (continued): Navigating New Territory

—-

"I've been thinking a lot about our future," Lee said, his eyes searching Liza's for any sign of how she might react. "We've always talked about our dreams and plans, but now that we're together, those conversations feel different. More... real."

Liza felt her heart skip a beat. She had always appreciated how open and honest Lee was, but this was a conversation they hadn't really had before. Sure, they'd discussed their hopes and dreams as friends, but the idea of a shared future was something entirely new.

"I know what you mean," Liza said softly. "It's like everything we talked about before is suddenly closer, more possible."

Lee nodded, his expression serious. "Exactly. And I want to make sure we're on the same page. I don't want to rush anything, but I also don't want to ignore the fact that things have changed. We're not just friends planning separate futures anymore. We're a team now, and that means we need to think about what we want—together."

Liza appreciated how thoughtful and mature Lee was about their relationship. It was one of the many things she loved about him. She took a deep breath, thinking about what she wanted for her future and how it aligned with what they had built together.

"I've been thinking about it too," Liza admitted. "And I agree—we need to figure out what we want as a couple. But I think it's important that we also make sure we're still following our individual dreams. I don't want either of us to lose sight of who we are or what we want just because we're together."

Lee's eyes softened with understanding. "I would never want that either, Liza. I want us to grow together, but also to support each other in our own paths. That's what makes us work, right? We push each other to be the best versions of ourselves."

Liza smiled, feeling a sense of relief and excitement at how well they understood each other. "Exactly. So, let's talk about it. What do we want for our future?"

For the next hour, they shared their hopes and dreams with each other, some old and some new. Lee talked about his career aspirations and how he wanted to eventually start his own business. Liza spoke about her desire to travel more, to see the world and experience different cultures, something she had always wanted but had never really prioritized.

As they talked, they found ways to weave their individual dreams together into a shared vision for their future. They talked about traveling together, about how they could support each other's careers, and even about where they might want to live one day. It was a conversation filled with possibilities, and by the end of it, Liza felt even more connected to Lee than before.

"I'm really glad we talked about this," Liza said, leaning against Lee as they sat on the couch. "It makes everything feel more real, more concrete."

"Me too," Lee agreed, wrapping his arm around her. "I've always known I wanted you in my life, but now I can actually picture what that life looks like. And it's even better than I imagined."

Liza felt a warm glow in her chest at his words. She had always known Lee was special, but hearing him talk about their future together made her realize just how lucky she was to have him by her side.

"I love you, Lee," she said softly, the words slipping out almost without her realizing it. It was the first time she had said those words to him, and as soon as they were out, she felt a rush of emotions—excitement, vulnerability, and a deep sense of rightness.

Lee's eyes widened slightly in surprise, but then his expression softened into a look of pure affection. He reached out and gently cupped her face, his thumb brushing against her cheek.

"I love you too, Liza," he replied, his voice filled with sincerity. "I've loved you for a long time, and I'm so glad I finally get to say it."

They leaned in, and their lips met in a tender kiss, sealing the words they had just exchanged. In that moment, Liza felt like everything was exactly where it was meant to be. She had found someone who understood her, who loved her for who she was, and who was ready to build a future with her.

As they pulled away, Liza rested her forehead against Lee's, a contented smile on her face. "I'm so happy, Lee. I don't know what the future holds, but as long as we're together, I know it's going to be amazing."

Lee smiled back at her, his eyes full of love. "Me too, Liza. We'll figure it out together, one step at a time."

—-

As the weeks turned into months, Liza and Lee's relationship continued to grow stronger. They faced challenges, of course—every relationship does—but they navigated them with the same openness and communication that had always been the foundation of their friendship.

One of the biggest challenges came when Lee's work started demanding more of his time. His job had always been important to him, but as he took on more responsibilities, it began to eat into the time they spent together. At first, Liza tried to be understanding. She knew how much his career meant to him, and she didn't want to be the one to hold him back.

But as the late nights and missed plans became more frequent, Liza found herself feeling increasingly frustrated. She missed the time they used to spend together, the little moments that had made their relationship feel so special. And while she knew Lee was doing his best, she couldn't help but feel like she was losing a part of what they had.

One evening, after another late-night phone call that ended with Lee apologizing for not being able to meet up, Liza sat down on her bed, her mind racing. She knew they needed to talk about this, but she didn't want to come across as demanding or unsupportive. She loved Lee, and she knew how hard he was working, but she also knew that they needed to find a balance if their relationship was going to last.

The next day, Liza asked Lee if they could meet for lunch. She chose a quiet café, wanting to have a serious conversation without any distractions. When Lee arrived, he looked a little tired, but he smiled warmly at her as he sat down.

"Hey," Lee said, reaching across the table to take her hand. "I'm sorry about last night. Things have been so hectic at work, and I hate that it's affecting our time together."

Liza squeezed his hand, appreciating his honesty. "I know you're working hard, Lee, and I don't want to make you feel bad about that. But I think we need to talk about how we're going to balance everything. I miss you, and I don't want our relationship to suffer because of work."

Lee's expression grew serious, and he nodded, clearly understanding where she was coming from. "You're right, Liza. I've been so focused on work that I haven't been giving us the attention we deserve. I don't want to lose what we have because I'm not prioritizing it."

They spent the next hour talking openly about their schedules, their needs, and how they could find a balance that worked for both of them. Lee promised to set clearer boundaries at work and to make more time for their relationship, while Liza agreed to be more patient and understanding when things got busy.

By the end of the conversation, Liza felt a sense of relief. It wasn't a perfect solution, but it was a step in the right direction. They were both committed to making their relationship work, and that was what mattered most.

As they left the café, Lee pulled Liza into a hug, holding her close. "Thank you for being honest with me, Liza. I know I'm not perfect, but I want to do better for us. You're the most important thing in my life, and I don't want to take that for granted."

Liza hugged him back, feeling a renewed sense of connection between them. "We'll figure it out, Lee. As long as we keep talking and supporting each other, I know we can handle anything."

And with that, they walked out into the afternoon sun, hand in hand, ready to face whatever challenges lay ahead—together.

—-

Episode 8

Episode 8: The First Big Test

The months that followed were a mix of highs and lows for Liza and Lee. While they had successfully navigated the initial challenges of their relationship, a new set of obstacles was on the horizon—ones that would test not only their commitment to each other but also their ability to trust and communicate when things got tough.

*The opportunity**

It all started with an unexpected opportunity that came Lee's way. One day, he received a call from a former colleague who had recently started working at a prestigious tech company. They were looking to expand their team and wanted Lee to join them. It was a once-in-a-lifetime offer—one that came with a significant salary increase, the chance to work on cutting-edge projects, and the possibility of moving to a new city.

Lee was thrilled. This was the kind of opportunity he had been dreaming of for years, and the excitement in his voice was palpable when he told Liza about it that evening.

"I can't believe it, Liza," Lee said, his eyes shining with enthusiasm as they sat on the couch together. "This is the kind of job I've always wanted. It's challenging, it's innovative, and it's a huge step forward for my career."

Liza listened as Lee shared the details of the offer, her heart swelling with pride at how much this meant to him. She could see how passionate he was about the opportunity, and she wanted to be supportive. But as she listened, she couldn't help but feel a pang of uncertainty.

Moving to a new city would mean leaving behind everything she knew—her job, her friends, her family. It would be a huge change, and while she wanted to be there for Lee, she couldn't ignore the fact that it would affect her life too.

"That sounds amazing, Lee," Liza said, doing her best to keep her tone positive. "I'm so happy for you. But... what does this mean for us? Would you have to move?"

Lee's excitement dimmed slightly as he considered her question. "Yeah, that's the thing. The job is in another city, about three hours away. They said I could start remotely, but eventually, they'd want me to relocate."

Liza nodded, processing the information. She knew how important this was to Lee, but the thought of moving away from everything she knew was daunting.

"Three hours isn't that far," Liza said, trying to keep the conversation balanced. "We could make it work, right? And we'd still be able to see each other on weekends."

Lee sighed, running a hand through his hair. "We could, but long distance is tough, Liza. And I don't want to put that kind of strain on us. I've seen what it does to people... I don't want that for us."

Liza appreciated his concern, but the reality of the situation was beginning to sink in. If Lee took the job, their relationship would change in ways they hadn't anticipated. And while she wanted to support his career, she couldn't ignore her own feelings of uncertainty.

"Have you made a decision yet?" Liza asked, her voice soft.

Lee shook his head. "Not yet. They gave me a week to think it over. I wanted to talk to you first because this affects both of us."

Liza smiled, grateful that he was including her in the decision. "I'm glad you're considering us, Lee. I want you to take this opportunity if it's what you really want, but we need to figure out how we're going to make it work."

They spent the rest of the evening discussing the pros and cons of the job, exploring different scenarios and how they might handle the challenges that came with a potential move. By the time they went to bed, they were both exhausted, but they had a better understanding of what lay ahead.

*A Decision made *

Over the next few days, Lee and Liza continued to talk about the job offer. They discussed everything from the logistics of moving to the impact it would have on their relationship. It was a difficult decision, but Lee knew he had to make a choice.

One evening, as they were having dinner, Lee finally spoke up.

"I've made a decision, Liza," he said, his tone serious but calm.

Liza looked up from her plate, her heart pounding in her chest. She had been dreading this moment, but she knew it was inevitable.

"What did you decide?" she asked, her voice barely above a whisper.

Lee took a deep breath before answering. "I'm going to take the job. It's too good of an opportunity to pass up, and I really believe it's the right move for my career."

Liza nodded, swallowing the lump in her throat. She had known this was a possibility, but hearing him say it out loud made it all too real.

"I understand, Lee," Liza said, doing her best to keep her voice steady. "I'm proud of you for going after what you want. And I'll support you every step of the way."

Lee reached across the table and took her hand, his eyes full of emotion. "I don't want to lose you, Liza. I know this isn't going to be easy, but I'm committed to making it work. We'll figure out the details, but I want you to know that you're still my priority."

Liza squeezed his hand, feeling a mix of emotions—pride for his achievement, sadness at the changes ahead, and love for the man who was so important to her.

"I'm committed too, Lee," Liza said, her voice firm. "We'll find a way to make this work, no matter what."

They spent the rest of the evening talking about the logistics of the move, discussing how they would handle the long-distance aspect of their relationship and how often they would be able to see each other. It was a difficult conversation, but they both knew it was necessary.

*The Move *

The weeks leading up to Lee's move were a whirlwind of activity. Between packing, making arrangements for his new job, and spending as much time together as possible, Liza and Lee were constantly on the go. They made the most of their remaining time together, going on dates, visiting their favorite places, and cherishing every moment they had.

But as the day of Lee's departure approached, the reality of the situation began to sink in for both of them. Liza found herself feeling increasingly anxious about the future. She knew they had a plan, but the uncertainty of what lay ahead weighed heavily on her.

On the day of the move, Liza helped Lee load the last of his boxes into the moving truck. The sun was shining, and there was a slight breeze in the air, but despite the beautiful weather, Liza felt a heaviness in her heart.

Once everything was packed, they stood together in the driveway, the truck idling nearby. Lee turned to Liza, his expression filled with emotion.

"This isn't goodbye, Liza," he said, his voice soft but determined. "We're going to make this work, I promise."

Liza nodded, blinking back tears. "I know, Lee. I believe in us. It's just... hard to see you go."

Lee pulled her into a tight embrace, holding her close. "It's hard for me too. But we'll see each other soon. And in the meantime, we'll stay connected. We've got this."

Liza clung to him, savoring the warmth of his embrace. She knew he was right—they would make it work, somehow. But that didn't make the goodbye any easier.

After a long moment, they reluctantly pulled away from each other. Lee leaned in and kissed her softly, a promise in the gesture.

"I love you, Liza," he whispered against her lips.

"I love you too, Lee," she replied, her voice breaking slightly.

With one last lingering look, Lee got into the truck and drove away, leaving Liza standing in the driveway, watching as the vehicle disappeared down the road. As the taillights faded from view, she felt a mix of emotions—sadness, fear, and a fierce determination to make their relationship work, no matter the distance.

* Adjusting to the Distance**

The first few weeks after Lee's move were tough. Liza found herself missing him more than she had anticipated, and the empty space in her life where he used to be was painfully obvious. They kept in touch through daily phone calls, video chats, and text messages, but it wasn't the same as having him there in person.

Liza threw herself into her work and spent more time with her friends, trying to keep busy and distract herself from the loneliness she felt. But no matter how much she tried to fill the void, it was clear that things had changed.

One evening, Liza met up with her friend Rachel for dinner. As they sat at a cozy restaurant, Rachel noticed the change in Liza's demeanor.

"You've been pretty quiet lately, Liza," Rachel said, her tone gentle. "How are you holding up with Lee being gone?"

Liza sighed, pushing her food around on her plate. "It's been harder than I expected, honestly. I knew it would be tough, but I didn't realize how much I would miss him. And it's not just the distance—it's the uncertainty. We're trying to make this work, but I can't help but wonder if things will ever feel the same."

Rachel reached across the table and squeezed Liza's hand. "I get it. Long distance is never easy, and it's normal to have doubts. But from what you've told me, you and Lee have something really special. You're both committed to making it work, and that

Episode 9

Adjusting to the Distance (Continued)

Rachel squeezed Liza's hand again, offering her a reassuring smile. "You're both committed to making it work, and that's what matters the most. Relationships aren't easy, even when you're in the same city, but I think you two have a strong foundation. You've been through a lot together, and you've always come out stronger."

Liza nodded, appreciating Rachel's words, but the doubts still lingered. "I know you're right, but it's just hard, you know? I miss him so much, and sometimes I worry that the distance might change things between us."

Rachel gave Liza a sympathetic look. "It's natural to feel that way, Liza. But remember, this isn't forever. It's just a phase, and you and Lee are strong enough to get through it. You just need to keep communicating and trusting each other. And don't be afraid to lean on your friends and family for support. You're not in this alone."

Liza took a deep breath, feeling a little better after talking to Rachel. She knew she had to stay strong, not just for herself but for her relationship with Lee. The distance was a challenge, but it wasn't insurmountable. She just had to keep reminding herself of that.

"Thanks, Rachel," Liza said with a small smile. "I really needed to hear that. It's easy to get lost in my own thoughts sometimes, but I know I'm not alone. I have you guys, and I have Lee. We'll get through this."

Rachel smiled back at her. "Absolutely, you will. And anytime you need to talk, I'm here. We all are."

The conversation with Rachel gave Liza the encouragement she needed. She knew there would be tough days ahead, but she also knew that she had a strong support system. And most importantly, she had Lee, who was just as committed to their relationship as she was.

—-

A New Routine

As the weeks turned into months, Liza and Lee gradually settled into their new routine. They made it a point to talk every day, sharing the little details of their lives just as they had when they lived in the same city. They set up regular video dates, where they would cook dinner together over video chat or watch a movie at the same time. It wasn't the same as being together in person, but it was the next best thing.

One weekend, Lee surprised Liza by making the three-hour drive to visit her. She was overjoyed when she opened the door to find him standing there with a bouquet of her favorite flowers.

"Surprise!" Lee said with a grin, holding out the flowers. "I couldn't wait any longer to see you."

Liza threw her arms around him, feeling tears of happiness prick her eyes. "I can't believe you're here! I missed you so much, Lee."

"I missed you too, Liza," Lee said, hugging her tightly. "It's been too long, and I just had to come see you."

They spent the weekend together, catching up on everything they had missed, revisiting their favorite spots in the city, and simply enjoying each other's company. It was exactly what they both needed, a reminder of how strong their bond was, despite the distance.

As they lay in bed on the last night of his visit, Liza turned to Lee, her heart full of love and gratitude. "Thank you for coming, Lee. This weekend has been amazing. It's just what I needed."

Lee smiled and kissed her forehead. "I needed it too, Liza. Being with you makes everything better. No matter how far apart we are, you're always in my heart."

Liza snuggled closer to him, feeling a sense of peace that she hadn't felt in a while. "I love you, Lee. I'm so glad we're making this work."

"I love you too, Liza," Lee said softly. "And we're going to keep making it work, no matter what."

—-

The Temptation

A few months later, as Lee was settling into his new job and adjusting to his new city, he faced a challenge that he hadn't anticipated. One of his coworkers, a woman named Emma, had taken an interest in him. She was smart, attractive, and charismatic, and she made no secret of the fact that she was attracted to Lee.

At first, Lee didn't think much of it. He was committed to Liza, and he made that clear whenever Emma tried to flirt with him. But as time went on, he found it increasingly difficult to navigate the situation. Emma was persistent, and while Lee did his best to keep things professional, he couldn't deny that the attention was flattering.

One evening, after a particularly stressful day at work, Lee found himself at a company happy hour. Emma was there, as usual, and she quickly made her way over to him.

"You look like you could use a drink," Emma said with a smile, handing him a glass of whiskey.

Lee took the drink, grateful for the gesture, but he couldn't shake the uneasy feeling in his gut. He knew that being alone with Emma was a bad idea, but he also didn't want to cause a scene by leaving abruptly.

"Thanks, Emma," Lee said, trying to keep the conversation light. "It's been a long day."

"I can tell," Emma said, her tone sympathetic. "You've been working so hard lately. You deserve a break. How about we grab dinner after this? My treat."

Lee hesitated, knowing that he should decline. But before he could respond, Emma placed a hand on his arm, her touch lingering longer than necessary.

"Come on, Lee," she said, her voice soft and inviting. "It'll be fun. Just you and me, no work talk, no stress. Just a good time."

Lee felt a wave of guilt wash over him. He knew that going to dinner with Emma would be crossing a line, and he couldn't do that to Liza. She trusted him, and he wasn't about to betray that trust.

"I appreciate the offer, Emma," Lee said, gently removing her hand from his arm. "But I'm actually going to head home. It's been a long day, and I need some rest."

Emma's smile faltered slightly, but she quickly recovered. "Sure, I understand. Maybe another time?"

Lee nodded, but his heart wasn't in it. He knew that he needed to be more careful going forward. The last thing he wanted was to jeopardize his relationship with Liza, especially over something as trivial as a coworker's advances.

As he left the bar and headed back to his apartment, Lee's thoughts were consumed with Liza. He missed her more than ever, and he knew that he needed to have an honest conversation with her about what had been happening at work.

—-

The Confession

The next evening, Lee called Liza as usual. They chatted about their days, but Lee could tell that something was bothering him. He knew that he needed to tell Liza about Emma, but he didn't want to worry her or make her feel insecure.

After a few minutes of small talk, Lee took a deep breath and decided to come clean.

"Liza, there's something I need to talk to you about," Lee said, his voice serious.

Liza's heart skipped a beat. "What is it, Lee? Is everything okay?"

Lee hesitated for a moment before answering. "Everything is fine, but there's something that's been bothering me. There's this coworker at my job—her name is Emma. She's been pretty friendly with me, maybe a little too friendly."

Liza's stomach tightened with anxiety. "What do you mean by 'too friendly'?"

"She's been flirting with me," Lee admitted, his voice full of guilt. "And she's made it clear that she's interested in more than just a professional relationship. I've done my best to keep things professional, but I wanted to be honest with you about it."

Liza felt a wave of emotions—anger, fear, and sadness all at once. She trusted Lee, but the thought of someone else trying to come between them made her blood boil.

"Have you told her that you're in a relationship?" Liza asked, her voice tense.

"Yes, I have," Lee said quickly. "I've made it clear that I'm with you and that I'm not interested in anything else. But she's persistent, and it's been making me uncomfortable. I just didn't want to keep this from you."

Liza took a deep breath, trying to calm the storm of emotions inside her. She appreciated Lee's honesty, but she couldn't help but feel hurt that this was even happening.

"I'm glad you told me, Lee," Liza said, her voice steady but strained. "But you need to be careful. I trust you, but I don't trust her. Just make sure you're setting clear boundaries, okay?"

"I will, Liza," Lee promised. "I love you, and I would never do anything to jeopardize what we have. I just wanted you to know the truth."

Liza nodded, even though he couldn't see her. "Thank you for being honest with me, Lee. I love you too, and I trust you. But please, be careful."

"I will, Liza," Lee said again, his voice filled with sincerity. "I'll make sure nothing like this happens again."

They ended the call on a positive note, but the conversation left Liza feeling uneasy. She knew that she couldn't let her insecurities get the best of her, but

Episode 10

* The Confession (Continued)**

Liza knew she couldn't let her insecurities get the best of her, but the conversation with Lee had stirred up emotions she hadn't expected. She had always trusted Lee, and she still did, but knowing that another woman was actively trying to win his attention made her feel vulnerable.

That night, as Liza lay in bed, she replayed the conversation in her head. She believed Lee when he said he wasn't interested in Emma, but it didn't change the fact that there was someone out there who could pose a threat to their relationship. It was a reality she hadn't anticipated, and it made her uneasy.

But Liza also knew that this was just another test—another challenge they would have to overcome as a couple. They had always been strong together, and she wasn't about to let her doubts or insecurities get in the way of what they had built. She had to trust Lee and trust in the love they shared.

** The Unexpected Visit**

A few weeks later, Liza received an unexpected message from Lee. He had some free time coming up and wanted to surprise her with a visit, but instead of telling her when he was coming, he decided to leave it as a surprise. The anticipation of seeing him again filled Liza with excitement, and she found herself counting down the days, wondering when he would show up.

On a quiet Saturday afternoon, as Liza was relaxing at home, she heard a knock on her door. Her heart leaped with excitement, and she rushed to the door, hoping it was Lee.

When she opened the door, there he was, standing there with a smile that made her heart melt. Without a word, Liza threw her arms around him, holding him close as if she never wanted to let go.

"Lee, you're here!" Liza exclaimed, her voice filled with joy.

"Surprise," Lee said, laughing as he hugged her back. "I couldn't wait any longer. I had to see you."

They spent the weekend together, just like they had during Lee's last visit. But this time, there was an added layer of intimacy between them. They had faced a challenge with the situation at Lee's work, and although it wasn't completely resolved, they both knew that their bond had grown stronger as a result.

On their last night together, they went out for a romantic dinner. As they sat across from each other in a candlelit restaurant, Lee reached across the table and took Liza's hand.

"Liza, I want you to know something," Lee said, his tone serious but full of warmth. "No matter what happens, no matter how many challenges we face, you're the one I want to be with. I'm committed to you, to us, and I'm not going to let anything or anyone come between us."

Liza felt a rush of emotions at his words. She squeezed his hand, her heart swelling with love for the man sitting across from her.

"I feel the same way, Lee," Liza said, her voice soft but full of conviction. "We've been through a lot, and I know there's more to come, but I'm not going anywhere. We're in this together."

They shared a tender kiss across the table, sealing their promise to each other. The future was still uncertain, and there would undoubtedly be more challenges ahead, but in that moment, they both knew that their love was strong enough to withstand anything.

A New Chapter

As the months passed, Liza and Lee continued to navigate the challenges of their long-distance relationship. They visited each other as often as they could, and when they were apart, they made sure to stay connected through daily communication. It wasn't always easy, but they were both committed to making it work.

One day, Liza received an unexpected phone call from Lee. His voice was filled with excitement as he shared some big news.

"Liza, I have something to tell you," Lee said, his tone almost bursting with excitement.

"What is it?" Liza asked, curious.

"I've been offered a promotion," Lee said, barely able to contain his excitement. "And here's the best part—they want to relocate me back to our city. I can come home, Liza. We can be together again."

Liza's heart soared at the news. She couldn't believe what she was hearing. After all the months of being apart, the possibility of Lee moving back to their city felt like a dream come true.

"Are you serious, Lee? You're really coming back?" Liza asked, her voice trembling with excitement.

"Yes, I'm serious," Lee said, laughing. "I can't wait to be with you again, Liza. No more long-distance, no more wondering when we'll see each other next. We can finally be together like we were before."

Tears of happiness welled up in Liza's eyes as she realized that this was the beginning of a new chapter in their relationship. The distance had been hard, but it had also brought them closer in ways they hadn't anticipated. And now, with the possibility of being together again, Liza knew that their love was stronger than ever.

"When do you move?" Liza asked, already making plans in her head.

"In a month," Lee replied. "I have to wrap things up here first, but after that, I'm coming home."

Liza could hardly contain her excitement as they talked about the future—about all the things they would do once they were together again. The challenges they had faced, the distance that had once seemed so daunting, all of it was fading away, replaced by the promise of a new beginning.

*Together Again**

The day of Lee's return was one of the happiest days of Liza's life. She met him at the airport, her heart pounding with excitement as she waited for him to appear. And when she finally saw him, walking toward her with a smile on his face, she felt like everything was finally falling into place.

They embraced, holding each other tightly as if they never wanted to let go. The months of being apart had been hard, but they had made it through, and now they were together again, ready to start the next chapter of their lives.

"I missed you so much, Liza," Lee whispered in her ear as they held each other.

"I missed you too, Lee," Liza replied, her voice filled with emotion. "But we're together now, and that's all that matters."

As they walked out of the airport hand in hand, Liza felt a sense of peace and happiness that she hadn't felt in a long time. The journey they had been on was full of challenges, but it had also been full of love, growth, and strength. And now, as they looked ahead to the future, Liza knew that there was nothing they couldn't face together.

Lee's return marked the beginning of a new chapter in their relationship—a chapter filled with new possibilities, new adventures, and a love that was stronger than ever. And as they stepped into that new chapter together, Liza knew that no matter what challenges lay ahead, they would face them together, hand in hand, heart to heart.

Episode 11 (End Of The Story)

With Lee finally back in the city, life for Liza felt like it was on the verge of something extraordinary. The two of them had been through so much—navigating the ups and downs of a long-distance relationship, dealing with temptation, and learning to trust each other more deeply than ever before. Now, they were together again, ready to embark on a new journey.

Lee moved into a new apartment close to Liza's place, and the two of them spent their weekends exploring the city like they were seeing it for the first time. They went to their favorite spots, tried new restaurants, and even started new traditions, like Sunday morning hikes and Friday night cooking sessions.

Their relationship was stronger than ever, and Liza felt like she was living in a dream. But this wasn't just a fleeting moment of happiness; it was the culmination of everything they had worked for, the result of the love and dedication they had poured into their relationship. It was a masterpiece—a work of art that they had created together, piece by piece.

One crisp autumn afternoon, Lee suggested they take a walk through the park. The leaves had turned golden and red, blanketing the ground in a tapestry of color. It was one of Liza's favorite times of the year, and she happily agreed.

As they strolled through the park, hand in hand, they talked about everything and nothing. The future was a frequent topic of conversation these days—where they wanted to travel, what kind of home they wanted to build together, and the dreams they had for their careers. But today, there was a different energy in the air, something Liza couldn't quite put her finger on.

As they approached a small, secluded area of the park, Lee suddenly stopped walking. He turned to face Liza, a serious but loving expression on his face.

"Liza, there's something I need to ask you," Lee said, his voice steady but filled with emotion.

Liza's heart skipped a beat. She could feel the weight of the moment, and her breath caught in her throat.

"What is it, Lee?" she asked softly, her eyes locked on his.

Lee reached into his pocket and pulled out a small velvet box. He opened it to reveal a stunning engagement ring—a delicate band with a brilliant diamond that sparkled in the afternoon sunlight.

"Liza," Lee began, dropping to one knee. "From the moment we became friends, I knew you were special. And as our friendship grew into something more, I realized that you're the person I want to spend the rest of my life with. We've been through so much together, and every challenge, every triumph, has only made me love you more. You're my best friend, my partner, and the love of my life. Will you marry me?"

Tears welled up in Liza's eyes as she looked down at Lee, her heart overflowing with love and joy. This was the moment she had dreamed of, the moment she knew in her heart was coming, but it still took her breath away.

"Yes, Lee," Liza whispered, her voice trembling with emotion. "Yes, I will marry you."

Lee slipped the ring onto her finger, and Liza pulled him up into a tight embrace. They kissed, surrounded by the beauty of the autumn leaves and the warmth of their love. It was a perfect moment, one that they would both remember for the rest of their lives.

After the proposal, Liza and Lee were swept up in the excitement of planning their future together. They began to talk about wedding details—where they wanted to get married, who they wanted to invite, and what kind of celebration would reflect their unique love story.

But more than that, they talked about the life they wanted to build together. They dreamed about the home they would create, filled with love and laughter. They talked about the possibility of starting a family, raising children in a home filled with warmth and kindness. They discussed their career goals and how they could support each other in achieving their dreams.

Every conversation, every plan, was filled with a sense of joy and anticipation. They knew that life would still have its challenges, but they also knew that they were stronger together. They had already faced so much, and they had come out the other side more in love than ever before.

Scene 4: The Wedding Day

The day of their wedding was a beautiful, sunny day in late spring. Liza and Lee had chosen to have a small, intimate ceremony in a garden filled with blooming flowers and lush greenery. Their closest friends and family gathered to celebrate their love, and the atmosphere was one of pure joy.

Liza looked stunning in a simple, elegant gown that flowed gracefully as she walked down the aisle. Lee stood at the altar, looking dashing in his suit, his eyes filled with love as he watched her approach.

As they stood together, hand in hand, exchanging their vows, it felt like everything had led them to this moment. Every challenge, every test of their love, had only brought them closer together, and now they were ready to embark on the next chapter of their lives as husband and wife.

"I promise to love you through the good times and the bad," Lee said, his voice steady as he spoke his vows. "To stand by your side, to support you in everything you do, and to build a life together that is full of love, laughter, and happiness."

"And I promise to love you with all my heart," Liza replied, her voice filled with emotion. "To cherish our relationship, to be your partner in all things, and to create a life together that is beautiful and meaningful. You are my best friend, my true love, and I can't wait to spend the rest of my life with you."

As they exchanged rings and sealed their vows with a kiss, the guests erupted into applause. It was a moment of pure joy, a celebration of the love that had brought them to this point and the future that lay ahead.

After the wedding, Liza and Lee settled into their new life together as a married couple. They found a cozy home in the city, a place that felt like a perfect reflection of who they were as a couple—warm, welcoming, and filled with love.

They continued to support each other in their careers, with Liza pursuing her passions and Lee making strides in his own field. They traveled together, exploring new places and creating memories that would last a lifetime.

But more than anything, they cherished the simple moments—the quiet evenings at home, the laughter shared over a meal, the comfort of knowing they were each other's safe haven in a world that could sometimes be chaotic.

Their lo'e story was far from over. It was just beginning, and they both knew that there would be more challenges to face, more tests of their love. But they also knew that they had something special—something that had been forged through years of friendship, trust, and unwavering commitment.

As they looked ahead to the future, they did so with a sense of excitement and anticipation. They were building a life together, one that was full of love, happiness, and the promise of a beautiful future.

Years passed, and Liza and Lee's love story continued to unfold. They experienced the joys and challenges of marriage, celebrated milestones, and faced hardships together. Through it all, their love remained strong, a constant source of strength and comfort in their lives.

They eventually welcomed children into their lives, raising them in a home filled with love and laughter. They taught their children the importance of kindness, respect, and the power of love—a legacy that they hoped would carry on through generations.

As they grew older, Liza and Lee often looked back on their journey together—the highs and lows, the moments of joy and the moments of struggle. They were proud of the life they had built, the love they had nurtured, and the family they had created.

And as they sat together, hand in hand, watching the sunset on yet another beautiful day, they knew that they had created something truly special. Their love was a masterpiece, a work of art that had been crafted with care, dedication, and an unwavering belief in each other.

The End

Don't miss out!

Visit the website below and you can sign up to receive emails whenever Soha Iman publishes a new book. There's no charge and no obligation.

https://books2read.com/r/B-A-AFSCC-QFVKE

BOOKS2READ

Connecting independent readers to independent writers.